Dream Castle

Have an adult help you remove the perforated sticker pages.

Random House New York

Copyright © 2005 Disney Enterprises, Inc. All rights reserved under International and Pan-American Copyright Conventions.
Published in the United States by Random House Children's Books, a division of Random House, Inc., New York, NY 10019,
and simultaneously in Canada by Random House of Canada Limited, Toronto, in conjunction with Disney Enterprises, Inc.
RANDOM HOUSE and colophon are registered trademarks of Random House, Inc.

Produced by Phidal Publishing Inc.
5740 Ferrier, Montreal, Canada H4P IM7
ISBN: 0-7364-2305-2
www.randomhouse.com/kids/disney
MANUFACTURED IN ITALY
10 9 8 7 6

The Grand Ballroom

Princess Aurora and Prince Phillip love to dance at the royal ball.
Use your stickers to get the party started!

The Castle Garden

Snow White loves to stroll through the garden with the Prince.
Help them enjoy a sunny afternoon with her animal friends!

The Royal Dining Room

Meals are always magical in the royal dining room!
Make sure the table is set for Belle and the Beast's special dinner.

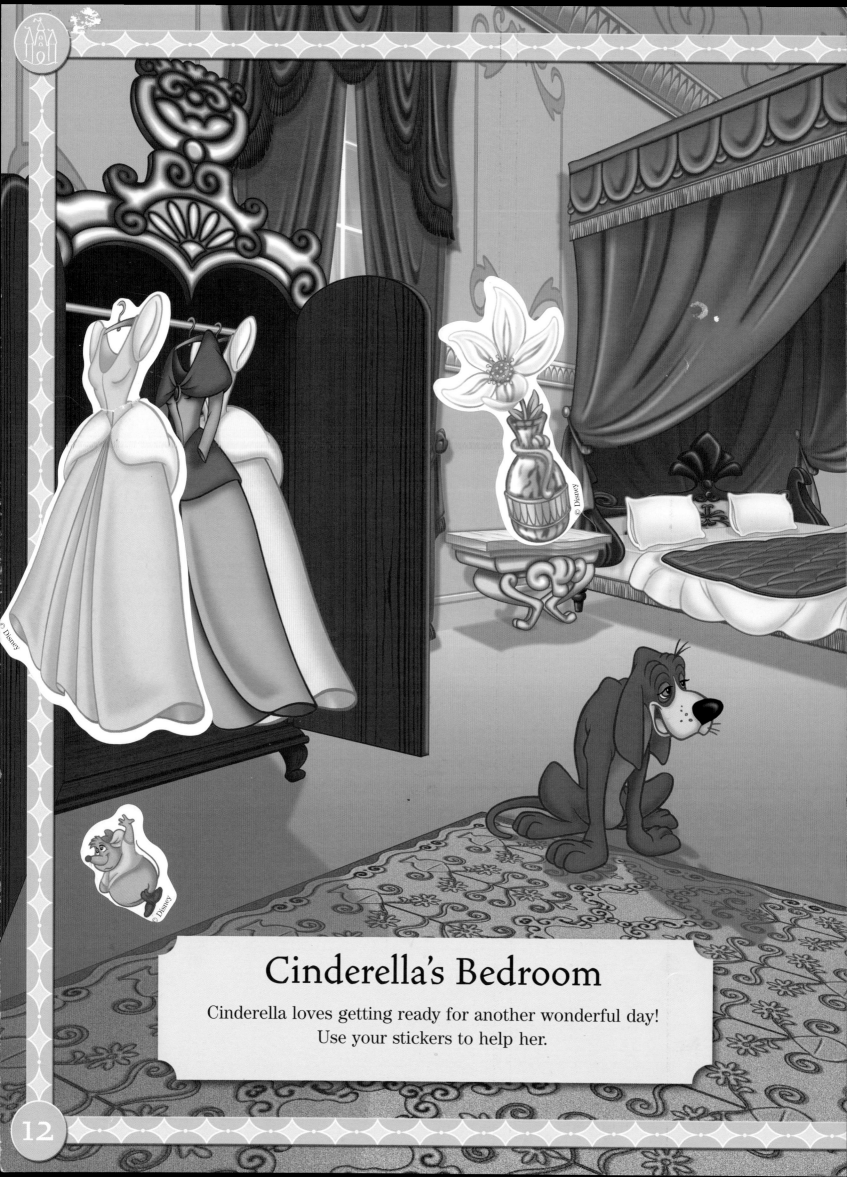

Cinderella's Bedroom

Cinderella loves getting ready for another wonderful day!
Use your stickers to help her.

The Balcony

Jasmine is ready for a Magic Carpet ride with Aladdin.
Use your stickers to help make their trip magical!

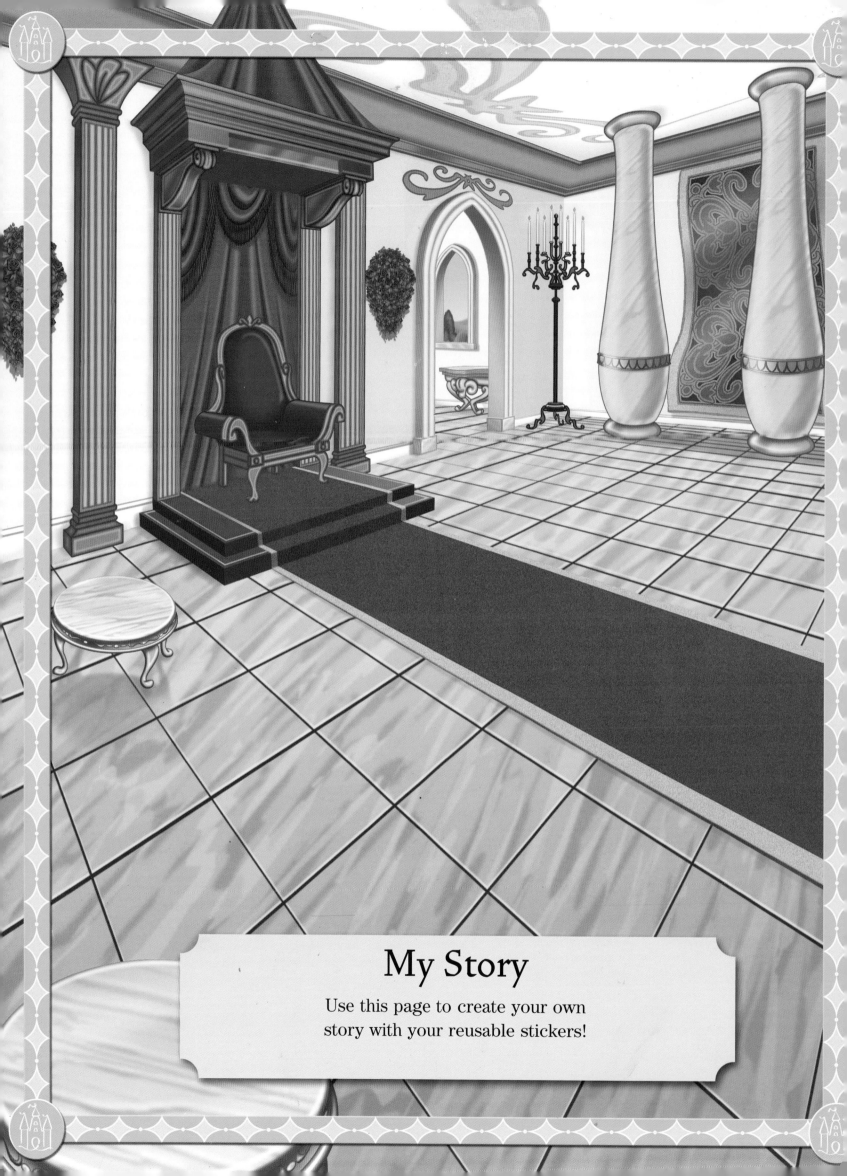

My Story

Use this page to create your own
story with your reusable stickers!